The Doctor's Inn 2

Still Practicing

N.V. Hill

Published by TaiLorMade Books

Chapter 1

As Brad looked down at the beautiful figure that lay before him, he couldn't believe that this was his predicament. He had finally found the woman that not only lit a fire in his spirit, but gave him a reason to believe that he could possibly love again. She gave him a new perspective of what true compassion was all about. Her humbleness and tender nature weakened him. RosaBella could have literally asked for anything she wanted and Brad would have gladly provided it for her. The only thing she had ever requested of him was to heal her son, which was a request that Dr. O'Donnell happily obliged.

Although Brad had never seriously dated an African American woman, he had always admired their rich melanin skin and their voluptuous figures. Brad grew up in an upscale neighborhood that was predominantly white, so it wasn't until he got into his medical practice where he was able to experience different cultures. By that time, he'd been dating Jenna who had also gone to high school with him. Even though they didn't get romantically involved back then, they kept mutual acquaintances. It was only natural that they would end up married.

Brad had no issue in making it known that RosaBella was his new love interest. He knew his issue would come once he made his family aware of how he truly felt about this woman. Obviously, Jenna had already made his parents aware of what was going on between them. Brad would just put it off by simply telling them he didn't want to discuss his personal affairs.

The men in Brad's family traditionally married women of the same race. They had black colleagues and friends who were invited over to social gatherings, but Brad had never known anyone in his family to date another race. Brad's parents were very prominent in their town. His dad was a surgeon and his mom was a high-powered attorney turned homemaker. He knew the time would come when he had to stand up for who he fell in love with versus what his parents expected. But now, he wasn't sure if he was going to even be able to have such a conversation. With RosaBella still in a coma, he wasn't sure about anything.

"Hello, Dr. O'Donnell," Dr. Joyner said, walking into the room.

"Oh, hey Dr. Joyner. I was just checking in on our patient."

"Yes...from what I heard you've been checking on her every day this week."

"Is that a problem?" Brad asked, getting slightly irritated.

"No, it's not a problem at all. It just seemed as if you were over concerned."

"In this profession, Dr. Joyner, I would be concerned when doctors stopped being concerned. I figured that's what a good doctor is supposed to do. I mean...she is my patient."

"Oh, well according to the records, her son was your patient. She doesn't even have a primary doctor on file."

"Well, now she does. Good day, Dr. Joyner."

Brad was pissed. Who was he to tell him about who he should show concern for? True enough Dr. Joyner was great at his practice, but he was a lousy, adulterous asshole who slept with every CNA or LPN he could manage to seduce by making empty promises. He must have been slightly attracted to RosaBella since he seemed to be around enough to notice when RosaBella was being visited. Although it was none of Dr. Joyner's business, he was in love with this lady and he'd be damned if he allowed an unethical, philandering whore stop him from checking on her health.

After a 15-hour shift, Brad went home and summoned up enough energy to take a shower. As the hot water splashed over his hardened six-pack abs, he thought about having RosaBella's back slapped up against the tile as he pushed his manhood slowly inside of her wet vagina. *Oh how wet she was*, he thought. He almost smelled the sweet almond scent of her shampoo in her hair when he would slip his fingers through it while ramming inside of her. To Brad's surprise, he wasn't imagining. He had accidentally grabbed the bottle that she had left over at his house a few weeks back. He shook his head and made a silent promise to do right by this woman if she made it through.

Chapter 2

Brad woke up the next morning earlier than usual. He continued to have nightmares about someone breaking into his home. He went to the bathroom and put a warm face cloth over his face to elevate his alertness. He thought he had heard heavy pounding coming from downstairs, but as soon as he turned the water off the pounding disappeared. He put on his slippers and walked down toward the kitchen to grab some coffee.

As soon as Brad had made it to the end of the banister, he was startled by an image through the stained glass of his front door. It seemed as if the person was just oddly standing there trying to peek in his home. He walked closer to the door to see if he could hear anything. He heard the voice of a lady on the phone. He quickly snatched open the door to encounter the last person that he wanted to see. It was his ex-wife, Jenna.

"What are you doing here, Jenna?"

"Why are you being so standoffish? I just came by to see how you were doing."

"Why?"

"Brad, we were together for years. You were my husband. You just don't stop caring for a person just because a few things go sour."

Brad took a minute and thought over her comment. Perhaps she was right. From his knowledge, he didn't have a reason to hate her now that they were officially divorced. She wasn't his problem anymore. Although he had no intentions of getting back with her, he could be cordial.

"Well, I appreciate you stopping by and I hope you enjoy your day," he said, slowly closing the door.

"Brad! Wait! Are you really not going to at least invite me in for a few minutes? I didn't drive all the way over here to get a door shut in my face."

"Jenna, I didn't ask you to drive over here at all."

"Please, Brad. I only want to come in for a few minutes. Besides, I have a few things in the hallway closet that I need to grab."

Brad thought about it for a second and reluctantly let her in his home. He did recall her having a few items still in his home, so this would be the perfect time for her to get them. That way, she wouldn't have an excuse to come over once RosaBella was able to come back and spend the night.

"Do you mind if I grab some coffee, too. I don't mind fixing it if you haven't already."

"No, thanks. I'll put a quick pot on while you grab your things. Like I said, I have to get dressed and get going, so I'll put yours in a to-go cup."

Jenna started looking around his home as she made her way back towards the closet. He was becoming slightly annoyed because he knew that she was looking for a sign of another woman's presence. He quickly prepared the coffee and set out the creamer for her to pour in and hopefully leave. She returned to the kitchen with a small make-up kit and one bottle of perfume. Brad knew that there were more things in that closet.

"You might as well get everything since you're here, Jenna."

"Oh, I don't really need that other stuff."

"Neither do I, so if you don't get it now, I'm throwing it all in the trash."

"Brad, why are you making such a big deal out of nothing? Aren't we able to at least be friends?"

It was clear that Jenna came to play games as she normally did. It didn't take long for her antics to turn into a nuisance. Brad grabbed a container and put the rest of Jenna's things in it. By the time he made it back up front, Jenna had stripped down to nothing but a thong. She bent over on the table and looked back at him.

"Brad, I know how you like it from the back in the mornings. How long has it been since you fed that thing?"

Brad's mind was telling him no, but his soldier down below was standing at full attention. Here he was alone with someone he was already familiar with and practically throwing it to him on a platter. Although she was mentally unstable, her body was still fit. It had been a while since he and RosaBella had been intimate, so he was very horny. Besides, RosaBella was still in a coma. Who's to say when she would pull through or if she would ever recover?

Brad walked over to the living room end table drawer where he kept his condoms. He opened the condom package and placed it on his hardness. He walked over to Jenna who was eagerly waiting for him to slide it inside of her. Brad grabbed her booty cheek and slapped his penis on her cheek. Just as he was about to enter, his medical emergency phone rang.

Stopping in his tracks, he hurried over to the kitchen counter and grabbed it. Brad knew anytime that he got called on the phone that he was needed ASAP. He briefly turned and looked at Jenna, and then turned back. He answered and quickly responded, "I'll be right there."

"I gotta go, Jenna, this is an emergency."

"I understand. Hopefully you'll understand and sympathize how I dealt with this for years. Perhaps we can finish another time," she said, seductively smirking.

Jenna put her clothes on, grabbed her things, and left. Brad noticed that she didn't grab the small container that he packed, but that would have to wait. *What did she mean that she dealt with this for years?* She was happy with him leaving as long as she had his money to spend. She acted as if it was his fault that she manipulated him.

Brad didn't have time to concern himself with any kind of reverse psychology she was trying to pin on him. He was excited and eager at the same time. He knew that this was the Universe intervening at its best. He ran upstairs, suited up, and grabbed his bag. This was the moment that he'd been waiting for. He had just got news that RosaBella was conscious.

Chapter 3

Barely getting parked good, Brad hopped out of his car and hurriedly entered into the hospital. Brad would normally go to his locker, grab a soda, and make small talk before putting himself to work, but he was on a mission. His colleagues greeted him throughout his hallway stroll as Brad threw up his hand and included a quick hello. His mind was focused on one thing and that was seeing RosaBella.

Once Brad rounded the corner to RosaBella's room, he saw that the door was shut. He wasn't sure if that meant she was resting or if she just wanted privacy. The nurse that called him had expressed that RosaBella specifically asked for him. This small detail made Brad comfortable with his decision to enter her room. As soon as he walked in, he was greeted with one of the most beautiful smiles he'd seen in a while.

"Good morning, Dr. O'Donnell."

Brad was overwhelmed with emotion, but he didn't want to show it. Although he hated feeling vulnerable, he couldn't suppress how much he'd missed her. He immediately embraced her with a tight hug while she was seated on the bed.

"RosaBella, I've literally prayed for this moment," he whispered.

He stood back up and attempted to get himself back into professional mode. He turned towards the sink and washed his hands in order to prevent her from seeing the tear that had formed in his eye. He side swiped it with his shoulder and grabbed her charts.

"Uh...the nurse told me that all your charts look fine. She said that you didn't sustain any long term damage and that you're practically fully recovered. We have plans to release you in the next few hours after a few more test come back. However, if you feel the need to stay longer you can."

RosaBella was dead silent. Brad turned to look at her and she was in a trance. He couldn't figure out if this was a side effect or if she was going back into a coma. He quickly rushed to her side and sat in front of her.

"RosaBella, are you okay? Can you hear me?"

She slowly met his eyes as the tears streamed down her face. He couldn't figure out what had happened in a matter of seconds. It wasn't long before she was crying out loud.

"RosaBella, what is it?"

"My baby..."

In all of the madness and excitement, Brad had totally forgotten that RosaBella was unaware that little Jeremy had survived. She had already taken the pills before he received the good news. He couldn't believe that no one had told her that already.

"Oh, no! Jeremy is okay. He's fine."

"What? My baby's okay? Is he talking and walking? Does he need anything? Is he-"

"Relax, my gorgeous lady. He's as happy as a one-year-old could be. I put him in a private shelter for temporarily incapacitated parents. They allow children to stay there for up to six months based on the doctor's recommendation and progress of their parent's recovery."

"What? You did that for me?" RosaBella asked, wiping her face.

"He actually stayed with me for the first three nights. Then, somehow child services got involved. I'm not sure how they would know that I didn't have a child, but it all worked out."

"Oh Brad! I don't know how to ever repay you for being here for us the way that you have," she said, squeezing him tight.

"Sweetheart, you two aren't an obligation. You're a part of my life now. This is what I'm supposed to do."

"Thank you for everything, Dr. O'Donnell," she said, easing her hand on his hand. "I truly love you."

Brad was shocked. Had RosaBella really just confessed her love for him? Was she really in love with him or did she love him for what he had done. Before Brad could respond, a nurse walked into the room.

"I'm sorry. Was I interrupting something?" The nurse asked, catching RosaBella with her hand on top of Brad's hand.

"No. I was just consoling Ms. Williams due to the fact that none of our caring and supportive staff bothered to tell her that her son was okay."

"Oh...I...uh...didn't think-"

"You didn't think that the mother of an injured infant whose life was almost taken by a stray bullet would be interested in knowing how her child was doing?"

"I apologize, doctor."

"If you could get our patient's charts and test results as soon as possible, that'd be great. I'm sure her baby boy misses her as much as she misses him."

"Yes, doctor."

After the nurse walked out of the room, Brad gave RosaBella a reassuring smile. He was immediately paged, so they didn't have time for further conversation.

"I'm sorry, Bella, I have to go, but if you need me for anything, call me, okay?"

Not wanting to leave, Brad gave her a wink and hesitantly left the room. Once outside, he took a deep breath and stood there for a brief moment. *RosaBella said she truly loves me. Does this means I'm supposed to take the relationship to the next level? Should I ask her to move in with me? Lord knows I've missed her so much. Does this mean I'm in love with her?*

Chapter 4

Several doctors were in and out of RosaBella's room after Brad had left. She wasn't sure if this was protocol or if Brad had personally sent certain colleagues to check on her. They were all being extremely nice to her while bringing her drinks and snacks that she didn't ask for.

After showering in her hospital room, RosaBella dressed in the extra clothes that were sitting on her chair. It was no question that Brad had put her clothes there at some point in hopes that she'd gain consciousness. Perhaps his hopes and prayers were what helped her survive. Whatever the reason, she was just thankful and elated that God had given her a second chance at life with her son.

Bella didn't get the chance to see the good doctor again once she was discharged from the hospital. However, he did manage to get her a **'thankful you're doing well'** card through a nurse. She understood that his job was very demanding, so she was fine with seeing him later that day or perhaps even the next day. Even though she was grateful for all that Brad had done, her immediate priority was going to get her baby boy.

The doctors sent RosaBella home with a few anxiety and depression prescriptions. They had suggested that she also seek psychological counseling due to the circumstances surrounding everything that had happened. They even added that she would be free of all expenses. Although Bella understood their concerns, she decided not to take their offer. She had surpassed all of her physical and psychological evaluations, so she had the right to reject counseling. Now that she knew her baby boy was alive and healthy, her life was filled with happiness and hope again.

It took no time for RosaBella to arrive at the shelter where Jeremy was. It was right around the corner from the hospital and a few minutes away from where Brad stayed. Perhaps Brad had purposely set it up this way in order to check on Jeremy.

RosaBella wondered if Brad was truly willing to accept her son as his own or did he help her out of pity? Surely Brad was smart enough to know had he not done anything at all that the chance of him being with him would be obsolete. However, he had to be interested in being with her in order to make the moves that he made. He didn't put her off as a crazed suicidal maniac and he stayed by her side. RosaBella had not ever experienced such loyalty from a man. She was definitely sure about what she had told Brad in the hospital. She was truly in love with the good doctor.

Not wasting another second, RosaBella got out of the car and entered the facility. A kind woman greeted her by name and checked her identification. It was no secret that Brad must have already called them and made the staff aware of her arrival. It was simple things like this that made her feel mushy. A few minutes later, a tall slender woman was walking down the hall hand in hand with Jeremy. Instantly recognizing his mother, the toddler ran toward her chanting "ma...ma...ma...ma." It was a tearful moment for everyone.

During the car ride home, RosaBella sang kids' songs to Jeremy while he gleefully bopped his head. Their reunion was magical. Jeremy only had a small scar from where the bullet had entered and exited. RosaBella couldn't thank God enough for bringing her kid back.

Bella unpacked Jeremy and carried him on her hip into the apartment. Although it looked as if Brad had gotten everything cleaned, a small dose of anxiety had run through her body. The memories of holding her child's bloody body began to resurface. She felt hot and trapped as if the walls were moving in toward her.

Bella stepped outside and took a deep breath. Luckily, little Jeremy thought it was a game since he was smiling and clapping his hands. There was no way she could stay in that apartment. She wasn't sure if she was going to be able to live there at all.

With Jeremy still on her hip, Bella walked back to her car. With the doors locked, she allowed Jeremy to play loosely in the backseat until she thought of something. Deciding to temporarily go to a hotel and stay, she left Brad a text message, asking him to suggest one that he'd recommend. Instead of texting back, Brad called a few minutes later.

"Hello, Bella? Are you guys okay?"

"Yeah, we're fine. I...just...I can't go back to that apartment right now," she admitted, trying not to allow her voice to crack.

"Well...do you really want to go to a hotel? I mean...there's plenty of space for you guys at my place."

"Brad, that's so thoughtful of you, but you know I couldn't intervene on you like that."

"Like what? I'd love to have you two stay over. We can...you know...make it a thing."

"Make it a thing?"

"Not like that, sweetheart. I mean...I would really enjoy your company and I could continue to bond with Jeremy."

It was music to RosaBella's ears, but she wasn't sure if she should accept his invitation. It was one thing to spend the night, but a semi-permanent stay would be imposing. She didn't want them to become a burden for him. Was all this happening too soon?

"Listen, Brad, I appreciate the offer but..."

"Then it's done. Give me fifteen minutes and I'll be over to help you get a few things."

As promised, Brad showed up to help RosaBella with clothes and a few other items. She could tell that Brad had been checking on Jeremy from the baby's excitement to see him. This helped Bella feel more comfortable about accepting his offer. After packing them up, he led them to his home. He explained that he had to return to the hospital, but he left Bella the key. He gave her a quick, passionate kiss on the lips and told her to make themselves at home before walking out the door.

Chapter 5

Brad didn't get home until the wee hours of the following day. Bella had slept with Jeremy in one of the guest bedrooms since she was still uncomfortable invading his personal space. Peeking in on the two, Brad couldn't help but to smile at the sight of his two favorite people. Thinking back on the fact that he almost lost both of them at the same time was frightening. He decided then and there to make plans for the three of them.

Quietly walking upstairs towards his room, Brad turned his main phone off and placed his emergency phone on the end table. Normally, he would be exhausted, but for some strange reason he had a burst of energy within him. Instead of taking a shower, Brad decided to put on workout clothes and jog down to the neighborhood workout facility.

About forty-five minutes later, Brad returned home sweating profusely. He instantly went up to his bedroom and stripped down to his bare nakedness. He turned on the triple shower heads in his master bathroom and embraced the pressure that penetrated his skin. As the hot steam filled the room, an invigorating sensation ran up the good doctor's spine. The gentle touch of a soft hand caressed his skin.

RosaBella pressed her naked body against Brad's from behind. Their bare skin bonding only intensified the moment. She put her hands on his chest and proceeded to hug him tight. She planted soft, seductive kisses on his back, simultaneously tickling his skin from the light scraping of her teeth.

The sensation was beginning to be too much for Brad to withstand. He turned around and met her gaze. As he stared at her angelic face, he cupped her cheeks in his hands. He placed a slow, romantic kiss on her lips. She instantly reached down and grabbed his hardness. She could tell he was ready to put himself inside of her.

Lifting her legs up and positioning himself between her, he slid his manhood into her openness. The smell of her hair and skin as he penetrated her openness had his penis throbbing. He placed his face between her jiggling breasts, licking her nipples as they bounced on his tongue. The gratification between the two of them was inevitable. Feeling the tingling sensation approaching quickly with each deep thrust, RosaBella exploded in sexual pleasure seconds before the good doctor released inside of her.

After washing up, Brad and Bella retired in his bed. Bella turned up the volume on the monitor that she had placed on Brad's end table in order to hear Jeremy. She put her head on the doctor's chest as he ran his fingers through her hair and massaged her scalp.

"You always know exactly what to do," she said.

"Nah. I think it's the fact that you make it so easy to be with you."

"I'd be selfish to take all the credit. Jeremy and I are blessed to have you in our lives."

"You know, Bella, I was thinking that maybe we could see how this living arrangement would work instead of you getting a new lease somewhere."

"Really?"

"I mean...yeah, why not? Jeremy seems to be comfortable here. I think it would be nice to come home to you two."

"Brad, I know you mean well, but I also know that it's a huge challenge raising a child, especially when he's not biologically yours."

"Bella, that's the silliest thing you could ever say to me. You were a stranger and I fell in love with you. What's the difference with loving Jeremy as my son?"

Bella raised her head and looked into Brad's eyes. Did he realize what he had said? This was the first time she had ever heard him say those words.

"Is something wrong?" He asked.

"Of course not. I was just wondering did you realize what you just said."

"Which part? Loving you or loving Jeremy as my son?"

It was all that Bella needed to hear. She couldn't believe that this was her new reality. She had her life back in addition to having the good doctor by her side. It could only get better from here. She hopped on top of Brad who obviously had the same idea from his ready stiffness. They made love again until the sun rose.

Chapter 6

A few weeks had passed and Bella was settled into Brad's house with Jeremy. Bella still had her money coming in from her inheritance, so she didn't work. Brad refused any money that Bella offered, so she made sure that all household items, groceries, and anything extra were on deck.

Bella still had plans to open her coffee and pastry shop, but finding the right location for the right price deemed harder than she had expected. Sometimes the location would be perfect, but the rental cost was too high. Then, she found an opening that was the perfect amount, but the location was on a busy intersection that most drivers would find troublesome entering and exiting.

After kissing Bella and Jeremy goodbye, Brad headed to work his shift at the hospital. Working hospital shifts was totally different from working at his office. The hours were long and there was no telling when Brad would get home. Although RosaBella had already been an at-home mom the majority of the time, she definitely wanted to do more. The daycare that she had Jeremy in before the accident was now full to capacity. Before she could make any moves, she had to find a daycare that was trustworthy.

While RosaBella was searching for daycares in the area, the doorbell rang. Jeremy was getting a well-needed nap, so she hurriedly went to the door. Once she opened the door, a skinny brunette in a tight fitting red dress stood before her. It was no secret who she was. Bella recognized her from the old pictures that were once in the home.

"Can I help you?" Bella asked.

"Oh, I'm sorry. I'm Jenna, Brad's wife."

"Oh, so you're the ex-wife? Well, I guess it was natural that I would end up meeting you."

"So, is my husband around?"

"Your ex-husband stepped out for the moment. I'll be sure to tell him you stopped by, but next time please do us a favor...call before you come to our home."

"Our home? Yeah right. Listen, Brad is expecting me."

"Oh, yeah," Bella said, dashing to the closet to get Jenna's left over items, "here ya go," she added, practically shoving the container in Jenna's hands.

"Tell Brad I'll be back to finish what we started the other day," Jenna stated.

"And we'll be right here waiting on ya," Bella said, forcing a fake smile as she closed the door in her face.

The nerve of that tramp, Bella thought. Jenna obviously knew who she was. Jenna had to envy her since the good doctor was now spending his money on her. Then there was the fact that she was now the epitome of all of his sexual desires.

Shrugging off her momentary pest, Bella went to the kitchen and grabbed a snack. She knew that she had put on a few pounds since her jeans seemed to fit a bit more snug. This was yet another reason why she knew she had to get out and be active. Sitting at home snacking with Jeremy all day was becoming hazardous to her health.

About a week later, Bella received a call from the owner of a few vacant buildings about five minutes from their home. The lady had advised her that she just contracted a shoe store, a hair salon, and dentist office that would all open in the upcoming months. She told Bella that she loved her coffee and pastry idea and had an open space for her if she was interested. Flabbergasted by her offer, Bella agreed to meet with her the next day, not realizing that she had also set up an appointment to visit Jeremy's possible new daycare.

The next morning she realized the error of her mistake. Luckily, the good doctor had appointments that could be handled by his nurse practitioner. He offered to take Jeremy to the daycare and meet the staff. Besides, Bella secretly figured that they'd be more inclined to treat Jeremy better if they thought he was a doctor's kid.

Bella had made a batch of her cinnamon frosted pastries to-go to help impress the lot owner. After picking Jeremy up to say goodbye, the toddler gave Bella a quick kiss, then instantly reached out for Brad. He held his arms snug around Brad's neck. The gesture made both of their hearts melt. After a loving goodbye kiss between the two lovers, Brad strapped Jeremy in his car seat and headed for the daycare. He had no idea that he was being followed.

Chapter 7

About two weeks later, everything was set into place. RosaBella's coffee and pastry shop was scheduled to open within the next four to six months. She decided to call it '*Rosie Pastries*' after her late mother. Jeremy was adjusting to his new daycare just fine and everything was going as planned.

The only problem was RosaBella couldn't get her right ankle to stop aching. She'd been wearing heels more often due to all the business meetings, so she figured that may have been the cause of the issue. However, when she started craving ice cream sandwiches and grilled cheeses for the past few nights, Bella knew that a pregnancy test was her next option.

Not wanting to alert the good doctor just yet, Bella went to the local drugstore and grabbed a regular pregnancy test and a digital test. She was extremely nervous regarding the results. She had obviously been having unprotected sex with Brad, so they both were aware of the consequences that followed.

Once Bella arrived home, she contemplated the possible outcomes. If she was pregnant, at least she was now in a stable and loving environment. She also felt like Brad would be a great hands-on father as he already was with Jeremy.

Bella also considered that Brad may have not been ready for kids at the time. He had just gotten out of a divorce and they were currently shacking. Brad generally seemed to be the traditional type of guy who wanted marriage first then kids. Even though they never discussed it, Brad may have assumed that she was on birth control. This made Bella even more nervous about the outcome.

After waiting five minutes, Bella went into the bathroom to get the test results. Just as she suspected, both tests were positive. She put the test in a bag and hid them in the closet behind her hair products. She knew that Brad would never look there. She had intentions to tell him soon, she was just trying to decide the right time.

With everything going on, Bella felt tired and overwhelmed. She had about two hours or so to pick up Jeremy, so she decided to take a quick nap. What seemed like an hour was actually about twenty minutes when Bella received a call from Jeremy's daycare.

"Hello, Ms. Williams. We tried calling Dr. O'Donnell, but we couldn't reach him."

"Well...I am his mother. What's going on?"

"There's been a small fire scare here at the daycare."

"Oh my gosh! Are all of the kids okay?"

"Yes, everything is okay. The children are fine and nothing was damaged. It seems as if water somehow got in the breaker. We're assuming one of the workers left a bottled water on top on the breaker since we found it lying on the floor. Anyhow, we just wanted you and Dr. O'Donnell to know that Jeremy was picked up by his stepmother."

"What do you mean? Are you joking right now? Jeremy doesn't have a stepmother."

"Oh...well...Dr. O'Donnell's wife came by. She showed us proof of the marriage license, so we figured..."

RosaBella instantly hung up the phone and headed to the daycare.

Chapter 8

RosaBella left Brad three frantic messages for him to pick up the phone and call her back immediately. Although she didn't blame Brad, she figured that he would have some idea about this woman's mindset. He was with her for years, so there would have to be some type of indication of a mental illness. She clearly had to be insane to deliberately take a child that wasn't hers. Once Bella arrived at the daycare, police were already there. She ran inside the building, trying to catch her breath.

"Where's...where's my son?" She asked, very exasperated and short of breath.

"Ms. Williams, we want you to stay calm. We have officers on the way to Jenna O'Donnell's home." The officer stated.

"She isn't his wife. The divorce was final months ago."

"We understand that, Ms. Williams, but she still goes by her matrimonial name, which is why the staff thought this was a legitimate move."

"How could this be a legitimate move when Jenna's name isn't listed on any of my child's paperwork?" Bella screamed.

"The front office manager was actually checking into that right before the fire alarms started sounding. His wife...I mean...ex-wife, convinced us that the doctor likely neglected to add her due to exhaustion. She had the marriage license with her," the daycare assistant explained.

"How? How could a piece of paper convince you? Was it because she's white? I'm his fuckin mother and I had to show my fucking identification the first time I picked him up!"

"Ms. Williams, we're so sorry...I can't begin-"

"I got here as soon as I could," Brad said, entering and coming to Bella's rescue.

"Oh, Brad!" Bella cried, rushing into his arms. "She took my baby! Jenna took my baby!"

"How in the hell could you let this happen?" Brad yelled.

"Dr. O'Donnell, we weren't aware that she was your ex-wife."

"It doesn't matter. She's not on the damn list!" He argued.

"Alright, Mr. O'Donnell, let's not start pointing fingers." The officer intervened.

"Are you a fucking moron? Of course they're to blame."

"Let's ease off on the name calling, Mr. O'Donnell." The officer stated, seeming to be aggravated.

"You're standing here arguing with me when my son has been kidnapped! Where's your children, Officer? Safely the fuck at home, right?"

The officer didn't say anything. He walked off as he began to conference someone in on his walkie-talkie. Brad continued to console Bella who was rightfully distraught.

"You guys better hope for the life of you that our boy is okay."

Brad escorted Bella outside to the parking lot. Although he knew Jenna could be erratic, he never expected this. This gave him even more reason to believe that Jenna was the one who shot Jeremy. Not wanting to further alarm Bella, he momentarily kept his thoughts to himself.

As Brad began to brainstorm, he already figured that even Jenna wouldn't be dumb enough to go back to her place. After calming Bella down, he explained to her that they had to take matters into their own hands. He suggested that he do all the talking just in case Bella's threats set Jenna off to hurt Jeremy. Trusting Brad's strategy, Bella agreed to allow Brad to do his thing.

Chapter 9

Deciding to leave the daycare, Brad and Jenna pulled into a local grocery store parking lot. They weren't sure if Jenna was watching them or if she had someone following them. Obviously, at some point she had to have been stalking them in order to know what daycare they were using. Giving Bella a nod, Brad called Jenna and put her on speaker phone.

"Hey lover, how are you?" Jenna casually asked as if nothing was wrong.

"Jenna, where is Jeremy?"

"Jeremy? Who's Jeremy?" Jenna asked as she snickered.

"Where's my son, you bitch!" Bella screamed, unable to contain her emotions.

"Oh, I see that you have your little Negro fling with you. That's good. Maybe now she can hear the truth."

"Jenna, where is Jeremy?" Brad calmly asked.

"I'll tell you where he is once you tell that trash the truth."

"What truth are you referring to, Jenna?"

"Am I on speaker phone? Can she still hear me?"

"Yes," they answered in unison.

"Tell her how you were slapping that dick on my ass a few weeks ago."

Brad looked at Bella and put his head down. Although he didn't have sex with Jenna, he knew he'd made a huge mistake. He definitely didn't think that something so minor to him would become this catastrophic.

"Tell her!" Jenna yelled, interrupting Brad's thoughts.

"Jenna, that special moment that we shared was undoubtedly sacred. Why don't we meet somewhere and talk."

"How do I know you're not just saying that?" Jenna asked.

"Because Bella and I were already on the verge of calling it quits. I only allowed her to stay with me because some gang members shot up her old apartment."

"Those apartments were trash anyway."

Although Bella didn't like it, she understood Brad's strategy. However, what was alarming was the fact that Jenna knew what apartments Brad was referring to. *Had she been stalking her this entire time? Was this crazy bitch responsible for the shooting of her son*? Bella sat back quietly and listened as Brad coerced Jenna to meet him.

After ending the conversation with plans to meet Jenna at an old timeshare cabin, Brad was at a loss for words. He felt as if he had led Jenna to believe that something was still there. Had he not had that moment of weakness with her, she may have gone about her business.

"RosaBella, I wasn't trying to hide anything from you. Jenna came over while you were in the hospital and I was feeling vulnerable. Several things were running through my head and yes...I almost had sex with her, but I didn't."

"Brad, my son is missing and I have no interest in hearing about you attempting to smash your ex while I was in a coma. I need my son."

Brad could tell by Bella's disposition that she was hurt, angry, and afraid. She gazed out the window as she did in the hospital before knowing Jeremy was alive. Not wasting any time, Brad came up with a plan. He knew that his only function in life was to get Jeremy back.

Chapter 10

As RosaBella sat in the car, Brad had pulled up to a pay phone and made several phone calls. She wasn't sure what he was up to, but whatever it was he had no intentions of being tracked. Everything was very secretive. It was almost as if he was putting a hit out on Jenna. *Was the good doctor willing to kill for her?*

Bella couldn't understand how someone in the doctor's circle could be so evil. *Weren't they all from a rich, upscale community? Didn't they have great childhoods and the best of everything?* While Brad was still stuck on the pay phone, he received a text message in his cell phone that interrupted Bella's thoughts.

Hey Brad. I think it's real shitty that you left Jenna for some black chick. Why would you want to be with someone who can't even get into our exclusive club without being interrogated? We used to joke about blacks together all of the time. Now what? And I'm willing to bet that you haven't taken her to see your parents. They'd flip. What a waste! Any who...while I don't agree with your ignorance, I also don't believe in the psychopathic shit that Jenna is doing. I was okay getting the black girl out of the way, but I'm not okay with kidnapping. Come to 155 Great Green Trail Suite 4T. He is here and he's okay. He's kinda cute for a black kid. Lol.

RosaBella forwarded the message to her and deleted it from Brad's phone. Her emotions were all over the place. She didn't think it would be this hard being with the good doctor. *Did he really love her or was it the sex? Were the jokes she referred to just jokes or racial slurs?* Perhaps she didn't know the doctor as well as she assumed.

It also became more evident to Bella that Jenna and her friends had been after her all along. She was that much more certain that her son's bullet wasn't a stray bullet. That bullet was likely meant for her. After Brad returned to the car, she told him it would be best if she stayed home while he went to see Jenna. She had no plans on telling Brad that she was going to get her son alone. As motivated as she was, she didn't need help. She was literally ready to die for her son.

Brad had also agreed that it was best if he showed up to the cabin alone. As crazy as Jenna was, she may go berserk if she saw them together after what he had told her over the phone. He promised to keep Bella updated as he set off to meet Jenna.

About 45 minutes later, Brad arrived at the old cabin where he and Jenna had vacationed on several occasions. He stepped out of the car with a dozen roses in his hands. As soon as he came to the door, Jenna was already eagerly waiting in a black push-up bra, thigh high fishnets, and black laced panties. Brad didn't trust her, so he urged her to walk forward so he could admire her from behind. Everything about this woman was fuckery. He was appalled that he had ever fallen for her. Even though he damn near hated her with all of his being, he had to play nice.

"So let's get the trivial things out of the way. You know that you can't keep that woman's son."

"Brad, I don't want any kids, less knowing her kid. Hopefully he'll be sold to the highest bidder by the weekend."

"What do you mean?"

"There's a guy on the internet that pays for lost or stolen kids. I have an appointment with him soon."

"Jenna, there's no way that you could actually think that we're gonna mend something between you and I if you do that. That child has a right to be with his mother."

"You know something, Brad. I'm not sure if I even want to be with you after you've been all over that trash. Perhaps... you don't even deserve me. Perhaps... you deserve something else," Jenna said, pulling out a gun.

Chapter 11

Brad didn't flinch. He knew that Jenna wanted to see him squirm or perhaps even beg for his life. He refused to give her the satisfaction. Besides, Jenna was the last person in the world he could imagine in jail. She wouldn't openly give up her freedom. However, after tonight, she wasn't going to have that option. He had a plan to get her talking. He walked over to the kitchen table and opened some wine as if she hadn't done anything.

"It's ironic that you still have that gun. That's the same type of gun that poor baby was shot with."

"What do you mean a baby was shot with this type of gun?" Jenna asked, thrown off by his valiant attitude.

"Jenna, don't play dumb. You shot through RosaBella's window and ended up hitting the kid," he said, sipping his wine. "Wow! This is the same wine that we had on our honeymoon night," he added, trying not to make her think he was only focused on Jeremy.

"Yes, it is that wine," she smiled, "but no...no, I didn't shoot that kid. I mean...there's no way that I hit that kid."

Seeing that the gun was of no consequence to Brad, Jenna placed it on the front room table. She walked over to the kitchen table where Brad was. His bad boy demeanor was intriguing.

"Why are you acting like you care anyway? You don't like black people, right?" Brad continued.

"I don't like that trash you're with, but I wouldn't purposely shoot a child. I thought I had shot her until I saw her leaving your house a few weeks ago."

"Wait. You've been sitting outside of my house, watching what I've been doing?"

"Don't flatter yourself, Brad. I came by to finish what we had started. When I saw her leaving your home, I was furious. You led me to believe that we were possibly rekindling something."

"Oh. Well, the cops are looking for that gun, Jenna." Brad lied. "We have to get rid of it."

"My fingerprints aren't on it. Besides, I had on gloves when I shot through the window."

Brad was excited that he had gotten her to confess multiple times that it was her who shot through RosaBella's window. It didn't matter if her fingerprints were on the gun or not, Brad knew that it was the same gun that Jenna's grandfather had bought her for her 21st birthday. It was even registered in her name. Also unbeknownst to Jenna, he had a recorder in his pocket. He decided to allow Jenna to incriminate herself a little more.

"You know something, Jenna, all of this commotion made me realize something. You'd literally kill for me. I guess that's kind of sexy as hell if I really look at it."

Jenna blushed. "You don't know the half of it."

"What do you mean I don't know the half of it? This is the wildest thing I've known you to do."

"You know...I never told you this but...back in college, I had that girl Tracy sexually assaulted. I paid off Gary Mumford."

"I wasn't dating Tracy. That was Ronald Dalton, or Daniels or something."

Jenna didn't respond. She had obviously gotten her guys mixed up. It did take long for Brad to realize that this woman was whoring around on him.

"Wait. You were screwing around with Ronald while you were with me?"

Jenna laughed. "It was college! We weren't even married. Who cares?"

Brad grew quiet. Memories of how he helped Jenna with his student loan money came flooding back. She had been unfaithful the entire time that they dated. Perhaps their marriage was also a scam. Brad recalled Jenna supposedly hanging with Ronald as friends even after they were married. He also remembered that poor girl being beaten and sexually assaulted. If his memory served him correct, that girl overdosed from drugs a few years later. Jenna didn't deserve to live and breathe as others. She was a demon. After a short, awkward silence, they both dashed for the gun.

Chapter 12

Easily overpowering Jenna, Brad grabbed the gun and pointed at her. Jenna pushed herself against the wall, exhausted from the struggle. Just like Brad, she wasn't fazed by his gesture. She began to laugh right in his face.

"What do you think you're gonna do with that?"

"Where's Jeremy?"

"I hope the little bastard is somewhere stranded in the woods with wolves."

Brad didn't say a word. He felt total disgust for this lady. The nerve of her thinking that it was okay to destroy people's lives was appalling. Brad wasted no time cocking the gun.

"What? You think you're supposed to scare me? You're a wuss and you always will be. Go ahead you little wuss. Shoot it!" Jenna shouted.

Seconds later, a team of officers busted through the door. Brad had almost forgotten that he set the whole sting up earlier when he was with RosaBella. However, Brad was in a trance. He was still focused on shooting this woman.

"Dr. O'Donnell. We need you to put the gun down. We'll handle it from here."

"She hasn't said where the child is," he said, still focused on Jenna.

"The child is fine. He is with his mother." The officer stated.

"That's right, you loser. Catherine called me an hour ago and told me that she gave the baby back to her mother. She doesn't want you. She didn't care what I may have done to you. She only cares about what you can do for her son. You're such a sucker."

Brad slowly lowered the gun and passed it to the officer. He immediately pulled out the recorder and handed it to the officers as well. He explained Jenna's attempted murder confession was on tape along with other incriminating evidence.

After giving a full report, Brad was allowed to leave. He immediately called RosaBella to check on her. She didn't answer. Perhaps she was overwhelmed by it all, but he wanted to let her know that Jenna would be going away for a long time. He tried calling again, but no answer.

When Brad arrived home, he noticed that Bella's car wasn't in the garage. He decided that he was going to go in and wait. Perhaps she took Jeremy out to get a bite to eat. After turning on the kitchen light, he noticed there was a note on the table. He picked it up and read it.

Brad,

We've been through so much together in so little time. You've been supportive, loving, and compassionate towards us both. What we've shared was something out of a fairytale, but like all fairytales, there's someone wicked on the other end. I'm not blaming you for what others have done. You can't control their actions. However, I can't help but to feel that some of your decisions or lack of have enabled others to act out accordingly. How could anyone take you seriously about being with me when we haven't been out in public together or I haven't met your parents? I can't recall you ever admitting to anyone that I was your woman. But even more than these minor issues, I can't continue to risk having my child go through what he's been through. He's not even two yet. I love you, Brad. And if you truly love me then you'll understand.

Brad picked up the phone to call RosaBella. He wanted to let her know that her letter was absurd. He wasn't hiding her from anyone. If anything, he was trying to protect her from the thoughtless comments and insults of others. He wouldn't allow just anyone to move in with him. He loved her and Jeremy. *This is some selfish bullshit*! However, the good doctor put down the phone. He had to look at things from her perspective. What if he had a child and people from RosaBella's past continued to hurt him or her? It wasn't fair for Jeremy. It wasn't fair for RosaBella. And at this moment, life wasn't fair for him.

Chapter 13

About a month had passed and the good doctor still hadn't heard from Bella. He reached out several times, but she didn't return his calls. He spent days on end wondering was she and Jeremy okay. He didn't want to believe that this was the end of something that was so magical. Yes, what Jeremy had gone through no child should experience. But what RosaBella failed to understand was that he was there for her through it all. Ultimately, the good doctor couldn't deny that without the existence of a romance with him, little Jeremy's life would be deduced to the minimal scrapes and bruises that he came into his office with when he first met them.

During his early morning shower, Brad had realized that he was out of showering gel. He remembered that RosaBella kept him stocked up on extra items in the bathroom closet, which was normally something he never did. While searching for the gel, Brad came across a bag that was tied together in the back corner. He figured that the gel could be in there, so he grabbed it. Realizing how light the bag was, he knew it wasn't the gel, but he had to explore his curiosity. Dr. O'Donnell quickly discovered that his runaway love was pregnant.

Pacing back and forth, Brad wasn't sure what to do. The love of his life was pregnant with his child and he had no idea how to find her. This was the good doctor's dream come true. Not only did he want a kid, but he was having a kid by the woman that he loved. Brad decided that desperate times caused for desperate measures.

Brad called in a favor to one of his patients he had delivered a baby for a few months back. She worked for different cell phone companies and helped locate where people were based on cell phone towers. She thought it was quite romantic that the good doctor was trying to find the love of his life. She even gave specific times when RosaBella was at certain places.

Brad discovered that RosaBella was living about fifteen minutes north from where he was. It was actually in an area where he initially decided to stay, but was influenced to do otherwise by Jenna. He also discovered that RosaBella was still pursuing her coffee and pastry shop. Illegally gaining the information from his source, he found out that Bella had a business meeting with her business partner at noon the following day.

Dr. O'Donnell was nervous as he sat outside across from the vacant buildings out of Bella's view. She looked so ravishing in her black and white pencil skirt and lime green blouse. She didn't appear to be showing just yet. Based on his calculations, she was probably a little under three months of pregnancy. Then, another terrifying thought arose in his head. What if Bella had an abortion? Could he ever truly forgive her for making that type of life changing decision without him? He quickly shook off his thoughts as he saw RosaBella shaking hands as if she was done with her meeting.

Without hesitation, the good doctor jumped out and headed towards Bella. The closer he got, the more nervous he became. He hoped that she wouldn't refuse talking to him. She had no idea what the good doctor was willing to do to win his woman back.

"RosaBella?"

RosaBella confusingly turned around until she saw the good doctor's face. He could tell by the expression on her face that she was happy, but slightly distressed at the same time. She was as beautiful as a freshly bloomed rose.

"Look, you don't have to say a word. Allow me to talk. I understand how you feel. I've constantly been putting myself in your shoes and I understand your decision to run away from me."

"Brad...I-"

"No, listen, my beautiful queen. You were right. I didn't step up like I should have. Even though I knew that you were strong, I should have thought about the fact that you could be vulnerable. Forget my family and friends, the world as a whole is against us. But I promise you, beautiful lady, if you give me a chance," he continued, getting on one knee, "I will spend the rest of my life fighting for us."

RosaBella put her hands over her mouth. She couldn't believe what was happening before her eyes. The good doctor was down on one knee in a tuxedo proposing to her. She had been hoping for a huge gesture from him, but she didn't want the baby to be a clutch. Wait. *Did he know about the baby? Did it matter either way?*

"Brad, I have something to tell you."

Brad took a deep breath and looked into her eyes. "If you decided not to keep the baby, I understand. I can't feel your stress and pain, and saying what you could or should have done is absurd. I can only empathize with you and nurture you until you're ready."

Bella's eyes were filled with tears. Realizing what she was about to do, the good doctor quickly took off his jacket and placed it in front of him. RosaBella bent down to meet his proposal.

"Of course I kept it and yes, I'll marry you."

From the Author

"Thank you for taking the time to read The Doctor's Inn 2: Still Practicing. I look forward to providing you with future entertainment that you will enjoy."

AND PLEASE...

If you'd like more quality fiction at this low price, I'd really appreciate a review on Amazon. The number of reviews a book accumulates on a daily basis has a direct impact on how it sells, so just leaving a review, no matter how short, helps make it possible for me to continue to do what I do. Here's a link to leave a review. Thank you in advance!

Customer Review

Feel free to check out the entire series as well as other books also available on Amazon.

Partially Broken Never Destroyed Complete Series

We Were Still Kids

The Doctor's Inn: A Private Practice

A Crime for Two

Alyce Leaves Wonderland

After Dawn Breaks

www.imadethebook.com

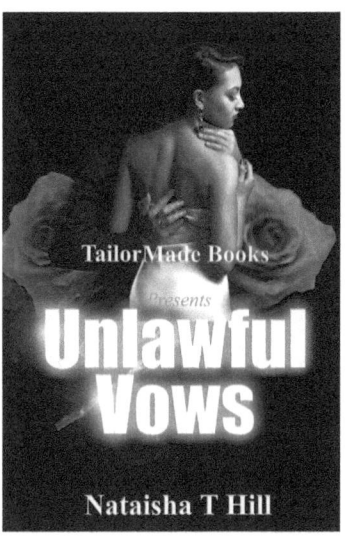

Prologue

"One less filth in the world," Sandra mumbled as she trembled so hard that it seemed the four walls of the basement were spinning around her. *Or were they*? She couldn't tell. She could only tell of the tremor inside of her. Her heart rocked in her chest, as though she'd been in a death race. She was visibly shaking. If she grasped an object, it would slither from her grasp and crash down into the floor. She was that unsettled.

Her hair, honey brown and wavy, was drenched with the sweat dripping down her caramel skin. If she wasn't stark naked, her clothes would be just as wet as her hair. It had been days since she last felt the comfort of clothes. At least proper ones. Lately, she was forced to go on without clothes, and when 'they' did let her get dressed, they only provided her with clothes that fuelled their sexual perversion. Vulnerability to the harshness of the extreme weather was nothing new to Sandra at this point.

It didn't matter that she'd been forced to forgo her skincare regimen for many weeks at a stretch. Her skin still looked radiant, holding its rich caramel glow. She was the true definition of a diamond in the rough.

Her knees buckled, seeking to give way as she stood on her feet. As if that wasn't enough to drive her back to the floor, there was the painful throbbing between her legs, where the man, her so-called master, had delivered a blow with his clenched fist. Now he lay nude and motionless, his life sucked out of him. His eyes were wide open, yet seeing nothing.

They were the same eyes that had always been brimming with lust and power when he took her, tossing her back and forth like a ragged doll. It was ironic how she'd strangled him with the very same handcuffs he'd restrained her with. *Poor thing*, she thought and smirked. He definitely hadn't seen it coming. If he'd known the chains of the handcuffs would bring him to his death, he certainly would not have introduced the handcuffs into his perverted game two weeks ago.

Sandra waited for the perfect time to strike. She waited for a moment when he approached her alone, with his wife nowhere in sight. Glancing at the dead man, her eyes were frantic to find the key to the handcuffs. Sandra had found it resting on his chest where it doubled as a pendant. She crouched beside him, yanked the key off his neck and unlocked the cuffs. The cuffs fell to the floor, clanking loudly. She bristled. That was way louder than it should be. She could only hope her boss's wife hadn't heard it.

Careful not to make a sound, she advanced toward the exit, but her plan to be silent was defeated when she mounted the stairs leading out of the basement. The wooden stairs, old and rickety, creaked with each step she took. Without the death sting of iron around her wrists, her skin could finally breathe again. *Freedom, Sandra. That's the smell of freedom.*

Sandra breathed deeply, filling her lungs with fresh air. This air was different. It was poles apart from the stuffed air trapped in the basement, or dungeon as she liked to call it. The air in the basement was rather foul, clogged with the smell of rust, sweat and of course…sex—if sex had a smell.

Sandra had no idea what time it was or what day it was. She'd lost track of time. She barely even knew when it was morning or evening, unless her boss approached her with a derogatory greeting on his cigarette-darkened lips.

The house was quiet, as though there was no sign of life. But she had a feeling her mistress was up there in the master's bedroom. She proceeded toward the stairs leading to the bedroom. Cold sweat dripped down her hair and trailed down her spine, until it found her butt crack. The air conditioner had her perspiration drying up in no time though. Her steps were unhurried, almost soundless, as she made her way to the master's bedroom.

She pushed open the door, her eyes straining to see through the darkness of the room. Her eyes adjusted to the darkness—it was nighttime, obviously—and then her gaze settled on a bump on one side of the bed. Sandra smiled. There Marie was, having her beauty sleep.

She lay on her side, her head resting on one of the many soft pillows on the bed. She'd definitely fallen asleep with the thought that her husband was down there in the basement having his way with their sex slave. Sandra edged closer to Marie and then she halted, her eyes devouring the woman.

She had no idea of killing this one. Marie looked…innocent. Naïve even. What if just like Sandra, Marie had also been sexually enslaved to the pervert? What if their marriage was one huge lie and she also needed saving? More questions crowded Sandra's mind, and then she sat beside Marie and touched her arm through the covers under which she lay.

"Mmmh," Marie hummed, adjusting herself on the bed. "Go shower, Carl. You must stink after being in that pathetic place for hours."

Hours? Sandra wondered. This woman was clearly exaggerating. *Was she drugged*? Perhaps she was too far gone in her slumber to think right. Her husband had only been there for a few minutes. Twenty at the most. He clearly had something even more sinister going on outside of them both, but whatever. None of that mattered at the moment.

Marie was silent again. She had obviously drifted back into sleep. Sandra concluded that she'd been right to think that Marie was naïve. Couldn't she feel that her husband was gone? Couldn't she feel that the person beside her wasn't her Carl? Seriously though, couldn't she feel that something had happened to him? Wasn't there a way these people felt these things? Unless of course, the movies and books were all lying. If this was a movie, she'd definitely feel that her husband was gone. Maybe she'd suddenly feel dizzy, or feel a sharp sting or a stab in her chest. Anything.

This woman felt nothing. She lay there without a care in the world, her chest rising and falling gently as she breathed. Sandra couldn't deny that while she hated every moment with Carl, she'd always looked forward to having sex with Marie. In those few months she was locked up in the dungeon, she realized a truth about herself—one she wished she'd known sooner.

She had a soft spot for women. There was a hole in her life that could only be filled by a woman, and Marie looked perfect.

So, she bent toward Marie and kissed her ear. She ran her hand up and down Marie's arm, and then she whispered, "Come with me. Let us leave this place."

Chapter One

Andrea smiled, her groggy eyes narrowing as a nose-tingling aroma made its way through her lungs. Sonny had made breakfast. Andrea could tell from the aroma that it was a heavenly meal. The man was a great cook, undeniably. He was even a better cook than she was. There was no challenging it. She could only wonder how great a cook his mother had been, since he'd learned everything from her. Sonny had the traits of an absolute workaholic, yet he always made out time to flaunt his cooking skills. *Show off.* That he was. But an outrageously handsome one.

"Rise and shine, beautiful," he said.

Her smile broadened. His sweet voice was the best way to start her morning. It was like a hundred violins playing in harmony.

"Good morning, handsome," she greeted as he stepped into her line of sight.

His face held a glow similar to hers, thanks to the soft smile stretching his beautiful pink lips. He was holding a foldable breakfast tray. The aroma wafting from the kitchen became stronger as he approached, causing Andrea's stomach to clench with a desire to be filled. He placed the tray on the nightstand beside him and then he sat beside her on the bed. Now, his face flooded her vision. She stared into his beautiful brown eyes—the eyes that had entranced her when she first saw them six months ago. It didn't matter that she'd lost count of how many times she got lost in his eyes—they still entranced her no less.

"Morning, beautiful," he stated, returning her greeting.

He lowered his head for what would be a kiss. She smiled, quickly turning her head sideways. She hoped that he wouldn't take offense to it.

"Morning breath," she quickly added.

"Nonsense." He replied and grinned.

She could tell from his voice that his cheeks, just like hers, were inflated with a smile. With her face turned sideways, he planted a kiss on her neck instead.

His lips stayed glued to her neck for a few toe-curling moments, and then he whispered, "Made you breakfast."

"Mmmh," she hummed, smacking her lips together.

When he detached his lips from her skin, she turned toward the tray, but he suddenly caught her lips between his. She chuckled, breaking the kiss, and then she raised herself so that she was slouching against the headboard of the bed. Sonny turned sideways to fetch the tray, and then he placed it on the bed. He'd made breakfast burritos.

"Oh my gosh, Sonny!" she exclaimed. "Thank you so much."

"For pampering you?" he asked. "If I don't, who will?"

He wiggled his brows at her. Her heart throbbed in response. *Gosh, he's so sexy. I can't believe he's mine.* His brows were so full, yet in shape. They formed beautiful arcs on his hazel eyes. That on his spotless caramel brown skin was sheer perfection. It was no wonder she always got lost in his eyes. It mesmerized her how a man could be so perfect without even trying.

His hair was dark and glossy. It was a little overgrown for a low-cut, but the heavy curls it retained were to die for. Andrea could do nothing but smile the whole time that he fed her.

"You deserve to be treated like a queen," he said. "You worked so hard last night."

He smiled no doubt because he was exaggerating. The previous night, they'd moved into their new home in an upscale neighborhood. But there'd been nothing hectic about the move because they'd hired a moving company to handle the whole process. Andrea had barely lifted a thing. The only thing she'd done was treat Sonny to a sensual massage. Her breath slowed as images from the previous night crowded her reasoning.

Andrea had skin of olive, contrasting with his honey golden skin. But that was where the whole beauty lay—in the contrast. There had not been better way to spend their first night together in their new home, and their twelfth day together as newlyweds.

"…you always work hard." He continued, feeding her another spoon.

"Not as hard as you," she said.

Sonny owned a technical computer servicing company where he made a six figure income monthly. So, if there was anyone who worked super hard, it was he. It was in fact one of the things she adored about him. That, and his sweet personality, had drawn her to him like ants to sugar.

As she thought about his job, her gaze suddenly rested on his white shirt. "Oh my gosh! What time is it?"

Her curious eyes found the clock on the wall. It took a while for her to focus in on the hour hand since the beams from the sun seeped through the blinds. It was a few minutes past seven in the morning.

"Sonny!" she gasped. "You should get going! You're gonna be late for work!"

"Chill, love," he said. "It's not like I'm gonna get fired or anything. I just wanna spend time with you is all…"

"I also want to spend time with you, love." She said, transferring the tray to the other side of the bed and out of his reach. "But we can do that when you're back from work. And besides, I wouldn't wanna mess up your beautiful white shirt…or crumple it…"

"And if I want you to?" He leaned in toward her and kissed her before she could say a word.

This time, he didn't give her a chance to remind him of her morning breath. In no time, his body was crushing hers, slowly lowering her to the bed until her back was almost flat against it.

"Know what? Fuck that office. I wanna spend my day with my beautiful wife." He started to undo the buttons of his shirt.

"Sonny, the tray," she reminded.

He rose from the bed and moved the tray to the nightstand, and then he returned to Andrea. His eyes burned into hers, and then he lowered his gaze to the rest of her body. She was dressed in a sleeveless silk nightgown, yet his gaze instantly warmed her skin. He unbuttoned his shirt. His pace was slow and calm. She wondered how a man could be so relaxed while his stare caused her to unnerve.

Her heart was beating twice as loud while her entire body had given into the surge of adrenaline. She could already feel warmth pooling at the depth of her stomach. His eyes undressed her, stripping off her gown before his hands even got to do so. She lay there in bed, watching him with a heaving chest. Her breath was growing raspy as wave after wave of adrenaline flowed through her.

Sonny tossed his shirt aside and then he rid himself of his pants right after. At five foot eight, he was just as tall as she was. Maybe only taller by an inch or two. Then again, she wasn't so crazy about the numbers. Besides, she found it more romantic that she could stare into her husband's eyes and kiss him without needing to stand on her tippy toes or tilt her head noticeably. Somehow, it made her feel closer to him.

Her eyes roamed his body as he approached her. She could not say that he had a ripped midsection, but he wasn't chubby either. He was just perfect—her definition of sexy. That was the one word she found most appropriate to describe him with. Her bone-straight, dark-root brown hair was now a mess. It was scattered around her head, tickling her neck as she lay there on the bed. But she was too lost in Sonny to move a muscle.

"I could stare at you all day," he said, staring at her in a way that made her feel flawless, as though she didn't have a litter of freckles on her face.

Unfortunately, he didn't have all day. The doorbell chimed in, bringing an abrupt end to their romantic moment.

"Perfect timing!" Sonny rolled his eyes.

The gesture was almost feminine. It made Andrea laugh. "I'll get it," she said.

Andrea had known the neighbors would likely come say hello to them. She just hadn't expected it to be so early. She rose from the bed and proceeded toward the door.

"Uhm..." Sonny began, clearing his throat. "I think you're forgetting something."

She turned toward him and wasn't surprised to find him holding her jacket. She smirked. "Jealous much?"

"Just for the cold," he said.

She could tell it was a little white lie, but there was a sliver of cold, so she could really use the jacket. His hands brushed her skin as he helped her into it. His hands left tingles all over her skin, making her crave more of his touch. She breathed deeply, her body aching for him in a way she'd never ached for another man.

Sonny was unlike any other man she'd encountered. Besides him being the only interracial man that she'd ever dated, there was something about him that drew her ever nearer, ever closer. He had a level of understanding that no other man could compare. That was what made her tick. If she didn't know better she'd say he'd gone somewhere for an intensive training on how to treat a woman right. *Such a heartthrob.*

"The door," Sonny's voice cut through her thoughts.

"Oh." She snapped out of her trance and headed downstairs.

Once she arrived at the door, Andrea looked through the peephole. A blonde was standing right in front, with her back to the door. Just before Andrea opened it, she took a moment to tie the belt of her robe. The blonde turned around with a smile on her face. She was apparently a few years older than Andrea. She was probably in her late twenties, just like Sonny.

"Hey!" The blonde greeted with her smile ever-so-present.

She had a bubbly personality—it was as evident as the fullness of the rack on her chest. Andrea had only just met her but she reminded her of her very lively best friend in high school.

"Hey," Andrea greeted back, flashing the woman a smile, but the smile was nowhere as excited as the woman's.

"I'm Heather!" the woman said. "And you're the new neighbor! I got home pretty late last night and didn't even realize someone new had moved in across from me."

She made her way into the house. Andrea stared at her, stunned that she'd stepped in so casually as though it were her own home. She shook her head, a small smile forming on her lips. The woman really did remind her of her best friend.

Heather froze in her tracks and then she clamped on her lips with her palms as she turned to face Andrea. "Oh my gosh! Where are my manners?"

Andrea chuckled.

"Pardon me," Heather said. "I'm just so freaking excited about having a new neighbor."

"I share your excitement, girl!" Andrea said. "Oh, I'm Andrea by the way."

She presented her right hand for a shake. She was unsure if this was the right thing to do. Maybe a hug would do it better, but she settled for a handshake instead. She gasped when Heather suddenly hugged her. For a moment there, it seemed like they were old time friends who'd just met each other again after forever.

"I'm so excited to meet you!" Heather said.

Although Andrea couldn't completely relate, Heather's excitement was pretty much visible in the tone of her voice. Her voice was high-pitched, close to a squeal. Andrea noticed how Heather's chest crushed hers, oppressing the moderate boobs found there—but in a good way. However, Andrea couldn't shake the fact that there was something eerie about this introduction. She couldn't put her finger on it, but something definitely felt strange.

Chapter Two

Getting along with the neighbor would be so easy. But then, there was the fact that the woman was sparsely dressed, and Andrea wasn't even the least cozy with that. Heather was wearing a red bikini top and denim shorts—very skimpy shorts that bared her thighs just as much as the bikini top bared her chest. Andrea wasn't so concerned about the shorts though—at least not as much as she was about the bikini top. Heather had ample skin on her chest. They were roughly twice Andrea's. Years ago, she would have found this intimidating, but a lot had changed about her since she met Sonny. He loved her the way she was, like she was the only girl in the world. And that was all she needed to change her view of herself.

Heather's top was having a hell of a time containing her twin mounds. It was a rather disturbing sight. Andrea glanced up the stairs. She could only hope Sonny didn't come down anytime soon.

Heather glanced around the house. "Is there anything I can help with? I can help you unpack, put things in order…"

"Oh, no." Andrea said. "Thanks for offering to help though." Heather suddenly grinned. "Who's the lucky man?"

"Wha…" Andrea started to ask, but then she trailed off as she found Heather staring at her left hand.

Heather's eyes were trained on the diamond ring on Andrea's ring finger. The ring held an eye-catching display of interlocking rows of diamonds and sapphires, with a larger piece of diamond mounted at the center.

Andrea blushed, finally getting Heather's question. "My husband is upstairs."

"Oh, I'd love to say hello." Heather's eyes suddenly brightened up as she glanced at the stairway. "Ah! There he is!"

Andrea followed Heather's gaze. She held her breath hoping that Sonny had made himself decent before heading downstairs. She only released her breath when she saw that he was wearing a beige t-shirt and black pants.

"Quite a catch," Heather whispered to Andrea.

Andrea blushed some more. She hadn't thought Sonny had heard Heather, but Sonny's words told her the opposite.

"Heard that," he said with a smile. He stepped into the living room, regarding Heather with a curious yet playful look. "I suppose you are our neighbor."

"Oui!" All smiles, Heather outstretched her right hand for a shake. "Name's Heather! I live just across from you!"

Sonny took her hand. "Sonny." He let go once he uttered his name.

"Well, Sonny, Andrea, it's a pleasure meeting you both." Heather looked from Sonny to Andrea. "My husband would love to meet you too, but he's one hell of a career man, always on business trips."

She smiled, almost wistfully, and then her lips parted to let out some more words, but the frantic howls of a dog was an end to whatever she was going to say. "Oh," she said, "Sandy is awake now. I guess I'll see you guys later."

"Thank you so much for coming over," Andrea said.

"See you around!" Heather waved them goodbye, and then she was gone.

The dog wouldn't stop howling. "Keep it down, Sandy!" The rest of Heather's words were lost in the wind as she stepped further away from the house.

Andrea leaned sideways, resting her head on Sonny's shoulder. "She seems nice."

"Totally!" Sonny said. "Glad you've made a friend, even though you didn't actually make an effort to find one."

"I don't need to." She wrapped her arms around him. "I have you."

"Aww." Sonny lifted her face with both hands and then he planted a soft kiss on her lips. "You know, I was actually thinking of getting you a doggie to keep you company while I was at work."

"This is not up for a debate, Sonny. You're getting me one." She playfully rolled her eyes, and then she suddenly remembered breakfast. "Oh my gosh… I gotta get back to my food."

She'd barely taken a step from Sonny when she heard the doorbell. She turned toward Sonny who'd plopped down on a chair a split-second before they heard the bell.

"Talk about some super caring neighbors," he said, his voice low.

Andrea chuckled as she gave him a playful smack on the head before going to the door. She found a petite woman staring at her with a brilliant smile once she got there. The woman was no less than twenty years older than she was, and the bold strands of gray hair on her head were an indication of that.

"Cookies?" the woman asked, grinning. She was holding a small basket of cookies. She presented it to Andrea, her laugh lines becoming more apparent as her grin broadened.

Andrea welcomed her offer with a smile. "Why, thank you, Mrs —"

"Penelope," the woman said. "Just Penelope."

"Thank you so much, Penelope."

"Call me Penny though. The 'lope' in it makes me feel really old, for some odd reason."

"Oh, Penny it is then."

Penelope handed over the basket. "Hoping you enjoy eating them just as much as I enjoyed making them."

"Oh, I sure will."

"What's your name, love?"

"Andrea."

"Well, Andrea, I'm the cookie granny who lives just over there." Penelope turned around and pointed at an apartment building. "Flat three is where you'll find me."

"I guess I'll be visiting you more often then," Andrea said.

"That would be great." Penelope chuckled. "I actually saw you moving in yesterday. I hope you like it here."

"Oh, believe me I already do. The neighborhood feels so heavenly."

"Careful though." Penelope's smile dropped as the words left her lips. She edged toward Andrea, and when she spoke again, her voice was the tiniest of whispers. "Green snake in the green grass." She added, glancing over her shoulder at Heather's house. She turned back toward Andrea and shook her head.

"Be careful," she said.

"Okay?" Andrea asked, an unsure smile crossing her face.

"…of home wrecking Heather."

Chapter Three

Such a bitch! Andrea thought. Penelope's words had been on Andrea's mind since their first encounter four days ago. There was no reason to doubt her. The woman would gain nothing from tarnishing Heather's image. So, the chances of her lying were as slim as the chances of Heather being a proper woman. Andrea sighed. She couldn't believe how naïve she'd been, letting a stranger walk into her home dressed like that when her husband was there.

The slut was on a home wrecking mission. That was probably why she'd visited. It had to be. Heather probably didn't even want to be friends with her or anything, Andrea slowly realized. She'd only come to check out the man of the house, and of course she liked what she saw. Andrea boiled with rage as memories from four days ago drifted into her head. She could vividly see Heather's face in her mind's eye. She could see her smile—a smile she would gladly knock off her face now—and that damned rack on the woman's chest.

"Gosh, I can't believe how stupid I was."

"Are you okay?" Sonny asked, his face etched with concern.

Andrea had been helping Sonny's feet into his patent oxford shoes, but then she'd slowed down as thoughts of Heather struck her. She actually hadn't realized she'd said those words aloud until Sonny asked if she was okay.

"Of course," she said. "I was just remembering back when I threw away some heels because I couldn't get them laced right."

She looked up at him, flashing him a reassuring smile. She was crouching beside their bed, just in front of Sonny who was watching her the whole time. She was still wearing the sleeveless white night dress she'd slept in, so Sonny was probably having a nice view of her cleavage from where he sat. Scratch that, he definitely was. She could tell from his now drooping eyes that he wanted to hold them and knead them, as typical of him. Her cheeks heated up as she thought of his hands all over her chest, rubbing her breasts.

Sonny was all dressed up for work, his torso enclosed in a formal white shirt, while a pair of dark brown trousers enclosed the lower half of his body. He was the perfect gentleman, his shirt tucked in so decently, giving an undisturbed view of his luxury leather black belt. Done with his shoes, she adjusted the hem of his pants and then she rose to her feet. He stood up as well, an arm encircling her slim waist.

"You sure you're okay?" He asked.

"Yes. I'll just miss you is all."

"Is this you asking me to skip work to be with you again?" He wiggled his brows.

"No! Of course not!" She feigned horror, and then she clapped her hands together. "Okay, okay. It's time to leave now."

She hurried across the room and picked up his car keys from the vintage coffee table. She returned to Sonny to place them in his right hand.

"Time to—" she started, but the doorbell cut her off.
Seriously? She thought. *It was barely even seven!* Andrea rolled her eyes. *I swear if it's that nasty bitch, I'm putting her in her place!*

"Maybe it's the old lady with some more cookies," Sonny said.

Andrea desperately wanted to believe he was right, but he wasn't. It took only a few moments for them to find out. Once they arrived in the living room, Andrea unlocked the main door. Heat flared up inside of her at the sight of Heather. The pathetic bitch was undoubtedly up to no good. She was dressed just as sparsely as she had on their first meeting.

"Hey Andrea," Heather greeted. "Good morning, Sonny," She chimed, waving at them, and although she had an innocent smile on her face, Andrea could see a gleam in her eyes that couldn't be anything but lust.

"Morning, Heather," Sonny said. "Sleep well, yes?"

"Of course," Heather said.

Damn it, Sonny. Please don't encourage her. Andrea thought.

"My car battery is dead though." She pouted. "I was wondering if you could…uhm…give me a hand. If that isn't too much to ask."

Her eyes were fixed on Sonny the whole time.

"I'd be glad to!" Andrea offered.

She feigned oblivion to a drop in Heather's mood, even though the drop was as noticeable as the sag of her breasts. "My husband is already late for work, so let's just let him leave and then…" Andrea leaned toward Heather and whispered in a rather chirpy voice, "…we can have some girl time!"

"Sounds great!" Sonny glanced at his Rolex. "Gotta rush."

He wrapped Andrea in a quick hug. "You take care, beautiful," he said.

When he tried to break the embrace a moment later, Andrea pulled him closer and kissed him. She made sure to let her lips linger on his. That should be enough to tie a knot in Heather's stomach. Andrea turned to look at Heather. The smile on the woman's face had morphed into a grimace. *Take that, bitch!*

"I love you so much Sonny," Andrea said.

"I love you more, babe," Sonny said. He gave Heather a small smile, and then he ducked into the front passenger seat of his black Audi.

Andrea stood beside Heather, her hands crossed over her chest. Heather's arms were folded as well. The two women stood side by side, neither one saying a word to the other. They watched until Sonny's car was out of sight. Andrea suddenly turned toward Heather, yanked her by the arm and glared at her. Heather gasped, her eyes widening.

"Now you listen, Heather Home Wrecking bitch," Andrea said, "I see what you're doing. I know how hard you're trying to get my husband to notice you."

"What?" Heather feigned oblivion. "Why would—"

"I'm not gonna say this again." Andrea clenched her teeth. "Stay away from Sonny! I've been through too many bad relationships to allow a hussy like you to ruin my good life. I am everything to that man. Besides, my husband certainly isn't interested in your saggy boobs!"

"Oh my gosh!" Heather gasped, snatching her arm out of Andrea's hold. "I can't believe that you would say this to me. You don't even know me. You just met me."

Heather's eyes were rounded with horror. If Andrea didn't know better she'd say the woman was truly innocent. But she knew Heather was far from it. Everything about her demeanor had proved it. Andrea smirked, knowing that her words had hit home.

"What?" Andrea asked. "You know you've been practically rubbing that unimpressive pair on his face. But really, saggy boobs don't move him. Sonny is a man of great taste. So darling, you best be of good behavior and know your place. Oh, and—"

Andrea clicked her tongue, her eyes roaming Heather's torso. She shook her head and then she reached out to move a lock of hair behind Heather's head. The misguided lock of hair had been trying to cover her left eye. Andrea didn't want that. She wanted to see the look in the woman's eyes when she spoke to her about her impropriety. She wanted to watch every word sink in.

"…just in case you ever need some proper clothes," Andrea added, "my house is barely a minute away."

With a smug smile stealing its way across her lips, Andrea turned away from the dazzled home wrecker and advanced toward her house. She felt accomplished.

"Someone has been filling your head with lies about me," Heather said. "It was that old hag, wasn't it?"

Andrea turned toward her with a smile. "Nobody had to tell me anything, darling. It's written all over your face."

"You don't know anything about me." Heather insisted.

Andrea's smile stayed plastered to her face as she stared at Heather and waved goodbye. She knew that was enough to tighten Heather's stomach with fury. So when she saw Heather's nose flaring, she knew she was hitting home. Heather didn't say another word. She whirled around on her heels, stormed off into her house and slammed the door behind her.

Over the next couple of weeks, Heather became non-existent to Andrea. There were no more early morning knocks or parading of that woman's body in front of her husband. The few times that they did see Heather was when she was coming to or leaving her residence. Otherwise, Andrea wouldn't have even known that she lived next door. The woman was a snail, retreating into her shell where she stayed hidden.

Chapter One

"Donna, this wedding reception is nothing short of amazing!" Kelly bragged, one of Donna's coworkers.

"Thank you, girl. You learn to appreciate the finer things in life when your man wants nothing but the best for you. I told you two that this would be a day for everyone to remember."

"Yeah, I must say it's hard to top three fountains of Moët and Gucci watches for the entire wedding party. Now, you just got to make sure he's able to perform since he's almost twenty years your senior," Anthony stated.

"Don't mind him...I mean her," Kelly said as she nudged Anthony in the side.

"Oh, you know I'm not. Anthony probably just wants to get laid by my man because he's run out of men to lay at the office."

"You're lucky it's your wedding day and you look too beautiful for me to roast, bitch."

Beautiful was an understatement for the new Mrs. Donna Carter. Her backless dress accentuated her curvaceous hips as the inseams of her white, sequenced gown pulled closely together to showcase her supple breast. Even Beyoncé herself would have been wowed.

"Excuse me...uh...Kelly, if you don't mind I have to steal my wife for a moment." Troy interrupted, gently waltzing his new bride away from them.

"Did he really just act like I wasn't standing here? See, that's why I don't like his ass."

"I'm sure his ass is the only thing you do like," Kelly said as she snickered.

"No, I am not being funny. He is a total homophobic and that's not cool. Before you know it, he'll make her stop hangin' with us. Yes, you too, bitch, while you're looking all sideways at me."

"Did you forget that we all work at the same place?"

"Duh, he'll make her stop working, genius."

"Donna is not that weak-minded to quit her job."

"With all the money he got he can buy her a new job just like he bought his hair plugs."

"Something is seriously wrong with you," Kelly laughed. "Besides, even if she did quit, she wouldn't quit us."

"Well, either way someone needs to teach him a lesson in manners and acceptance."

"Calm down, Anthony. Don't get your panties in a bunch from over thinking. It could have been a simple oversight. He probably just didn't remember you."

"Bitch, no one forgets the queen. And for your info, I'm not wearing any panties."

"You are so nasty."

"Bitch, you don't know the half of it. Now, let's go get some drinks furbished by Mr. Anti-Homely himself."

Donna followed her husband, noticing that he had a tight squeeze on her hand. Observing that he didn't even acknowledge Anthony, this was probably going to be a brief spill about him being there. Donna didn't care. She knew her friends before she even met Troy, so she refused to let him dictate her relationships.

"What is that thing doing here?" Troy asked as they mingled on the dance floor.

"That is very disrespectful. Anthony is my friend," Donna stated, slightly agitated.

"Whatever it is; I told you that I didn't want it at my wedding."

"This isn't the wedding, it's the reception, and since when did you think that you were going to be able to choose my friends?"

"Thy shall not be disobedient to thine husband."

"Exactly. You are my husband, not my father."

"Perhaps someone should have been your father and taught you right from wrong."

"Are you really doing this on our wedding night?"

"Look, I have a business meeting in about an hour and a half. Finish up with your little friends, so we can still make our flight and I can spoil you in the Caribbean." He said, kissing her on the forehead and walking off to greet his daughter who was waving from the other side of the room to get his attention.

Donna hated when Troy would try to start an argument and then throw something extravagant in her face so that she wouldn't press the issue. Donna had expressed to Troy early on in the relationship that her mother and father both died in a car accident when she was seven. She went from foster home to foster home and the journey was beyond horrifying.

Although Troy sometimes had the jerkiest attitude about things, he treated her like a princess. Money wasn't an object since he was the carpeting tycoon of south Arizona. Besides, she was head-over-hills in love with Troy and would do just about anything to please him.

Troy was older and wasn't as physically active as Donna, but his magic stick still did the trick most of the time. The only drawback was that he couldn't last long unless he took Viagra, which ultimately gave him bad migraines.

Donna sometimes found herself pretending during sex, but Troy was the master at giving oral, which compensated for his stamina shortage. For a middle-aged man he was still very handsome and adventurous. He was actually about a ninety percent upgrade from all the other losers she had dated, so his minor flaws were acceptable.

The only other problem that Donna had was that she didn't like how Troy allowed his daughter to treat her. The nerve of her, Donna thought. Who allows their child to not only be absent from the wedding, but to show up at the reception and not speak? Now that Donna was officially moving into Troy's mansion, Monica had no choice but to abide by her rules whenever she came over to visit. She may not ever acknowledge her as her stepmother, but she sure in the hell was going to respect her as one.

"Monica, I'm glad you decided to come. I see you've changed your mind about your stepmother." Troy said, walking over to embrace his daughter Monica.

"Dad, she's not my mother. She's only about six or seven years older than me. Did you tell mom about the marriage?"

"Age is not defined with love, yet love is graced by infinite passion in youth," he said, totally ignoring her question.

"Yeah...sure, dad. I find it very convenient for a young office assistant to marry a rich mogul who technically could be her dad."

"Outside of love, the benefit of a union should go both ways. You would know that if you didn't have that son-of-a-bitch boyfriend leeching off of you."

"Dad, Eric is trying to open up his own fitness center. How is that leeching?"

"When was the last time he bought you something or paid for a date?"

"Dad, this isn't the time to discuss this. Listen, I need you to wire a thousand dollars in my account."

"Have you spoken to Donna yet?" He asked, totally ignoring her request.

"I was gonna-"

"So you have the guts to ask me for money on my wedding day, but you haven't even spoken to my wife?"

"I'm going now, dad. Could you wire the money now? Please and thank you." She added, walking over towards Donna.

"Hi, Donna. I came to say congratulations and you look nice." Monica stated, in the driest tone.

"Oh, is this your way of trying to act decent or did someone offer you some kind of incentive to talk to me."

"You know...whatever, Donna. You think you know everything, but you're no smarter than I am. We could have practically been in the same school together at some point."

"And it just burns you up that I'm the new apple of your daddy's eyes, doesn't it?

"Be careful what you say to me, Donna. You should always remember that I'll always be his daughter."

"That may be true, but now that we're married, I will always have access to the finances. I suggest you play nice. You wouldn't want the rent on your apartment to accidentally get defaulted."

As Monica walked off with a mean glare on her face, Donna knew that dealing with her was going to be challenging. She was the youngest daughter of her husband's two girls, so he had spoiled her rotten. Perhaps, Troy's missing ex-wife played a role in Monica's lack of respect for her.

Donna found it quite strange that she up and left the kids after the divorce. Although they were grown, it would seem as if she would at least stay in contact with her kids. Almost a year had passed and they heard nothing from her.

According to Troy, their mother did send them gifts with no return address for their birthdays and Christmas. Troy claimed that he loaned their mom some money before she left because she wanted to explore the world with her new friend guy. He also told the girls that their mom still randomly calls him from a private number to check on them. Donna just figured that she had a mental breakdown after the divorce and needed time to find herself. As selfish as it was, their mother being gone was one less person she had to deal with when it came to Troy.

"Drive!" Monica demanded to her boyfriend Eric, who was sitting in the car.

"What's your problem?"

"I literally hate that bitch!"

"Babe, that's his wife. You two are gonna have to find a way to get along."

"Not if I can help it."

"Babe, what are you plotting in that big, pretty head of yours?"

"Don't worry about it, Eric Bernard Ferguson."

"Hey! What did I tell you about calling me by my full name," he quickly said, playfully poking her in the neck.

"Stop!" She complained. "You're so annoying."

"And you're too damn sensitive. You need to just stay out of your dad's and Donna's business."

"Shut up and drive. I'm almost tempted to get rid of you just like I'm going to get rid of dirty Donna."

We Were Still Kids (Sample)

Charlie and Joey stood stiff as they looked at Jodie in awe. Joey was young enough to go for it, but Charlie was skeptical. She couldn't believe that Jodie was falling for it, too.

"He's a liar. How would he know our parents?" Charlie asked.

"Well, he asked me who did we stay with, and when I told him Grandma Rose, he said 'yeah, I know your parents. Y'all are those Johnson kids' and I hadn't told him anything," Jodie explained.

"Well, duh, that's my teacher, so I'm sure it wouldn't be hard for him to remember my last name," Charlie said in a matter-of-fact tone.

"Everybody knows he's just a temporary replacement for Ms. Kindle," teased Jodie.

"So?"

"So…what makes you think you're so special that he learned your last name in one day?"

"At least I don't believe everything I hear. You're more gullible than Joey and he's the youngest."

"And you're just mad he told me about mom and not you because he thinks I'm the pretty one," Jodie snapped back.

"Yeah, pretty ugly," Joey said, playfully pushing Jodie's arm and running towards the porch.

As Jodie ran after him towards the house, Charlie's feelings were hurt. Not because of what Jodie said about their looks; Charlie already knew Jodie was prettier than her. Charlie just didn't think that Mr. Frye would like Jodie more than he liked her.

About an hour or so later grandma had arrived home from work. Charlie was sitting in the front room sulking. She tried to hide her feelings, but she clearly wasn't good at it.

"Pick your face up, girl, before somebody step on it," said Grandma Rose as she walked toward the kitchen.

"Yes, grandma," she softly replied.

"What's the matter with you, Charlie?"

Charlie knew she couldn't hide anything from her grandma, but she didn't want to tell her what was bothering her. Charlie figured she'd whip her butt if she told her grandmother she was sad over something silly such as not being favored by a teacher.

"Everything was going fine until I got to homeroom this morning. We got a new teacher, grandma, and I'm not sure if things will work out," she finally said.

"Oh, it'll be okay, Charlie, I'm sure your teacher will like you just as much as the old teacher did. Now, go wash up for dinner."

"Ok, grandma."

Later that evening, Charlie quietly sat down at the dinner table and kept her mouth full, so she didn't have to do a lot of talking. Grandma told the others Charlie was upset because her old teacher was gone, but Jodie knew better. She knew she had crossed the line. Charlie could tell Jodie felt bad from the way she put her head down every time Charlie looked across the table at her.

After dinner, grandma made them clean up and get ready for bed. Joey had to get his hair brushed every night, so his eczema wouldn't flare up on his scalp. This gave Jodie a little time to talk to Charlie alone. She gave Charlie a push as they hopped in the bed.

"Are u still mad at me?" Jodie asked.

"No, who could stay mad at the prettiest girl in the world."

"Come on, really, Charlie? I didn't mean anything by it, besides; you are my sister, so you look just like me."

"I'm flattered," Charlie said, forging a fake smile.

"Come on, are we cool again, or do I have to call u a pretty toad for the rest of the week?"

They both started to laugh. They laughed so hard that grandma yelled to the back, giving them a warning as they scrambled to get in the bed. Feeling better, Charlie lay down and began to daydream about things she wanted to do on summer break.

"I love you, Charlie poop," Jodie said.

"I love you, too, beautiful toad," responded Charlie with a soft giggle and then they were both fast asleep.

It was finally Friday and the kids were happy that the weekend was approaching. Charlie wasn't as enthusiastic about her new teacher as she was the day before. She couldn't help but think he liked Jodie more than he did her. Jodie wasn't smarter than her or as funny as her. Jodie was only prettier than her and not by much. Charlie knew that teachers had their favorites, but good Lord; Jodie wasn't even in Mr. Frye's class. Maybe he just told Jodie about mom because she was older and assumed Jodie would better understand whatever he told her. On the other hand, Charlie knew it didn't matter because whatever he told Jodie about mom, Jodie would tell her.

Once school was over, Charlie went to meet up with Jodie and Joey outside by the school gymnasium. By the time she rounded the corner, she saw one of Joey's teachers standing with them with a big brown bag in her hand.

"Hey Charlie!" Jodie said as she ran up to her. "Guess what?"

"What?"

"Joey won the brown bag special in his class today!"

"What's the brown bag special?"

"It's fresh tomatoes, bell peppers, onions, carrots, and potatoes from Ms. Noel's garden."

Ms. Noel was the fourth-grade science teacher who had a green thumb. She would sporadically bring vegetables and fruits to school and one lucky kid in her class would win the collection in a drawing. Science was the only class Joey liked, so it was no surprise when he won.

Almost as if he had heard his name, Mr. Frye walked around the corner swinging his keys around his finger. Charlie began to wonder was he following them around the school. Why did he just seem to pop up when they were all together? Mr. Frye's humorous persona soon began to turn into annoyance.

"Hey kids. I found out in the teachers' lounge that little Joey won the brown bag surprise. Congratulations, sport!" He said, rubbing Joey's head.

"Yeah, I'm normally always in trouble, but not this time," Joey gleamed.

"Well, I'll be more than happy to give you guys a lift," offered Mr. Frye.

"No, we're taking the bus," blurted Charlie.

"Charlie, that's not polite. Sure, Mr. Frye, just drop us off where you left us the other day."

"Will do, I just have to stop by my house first."

"Jodie, you know grandma ain't about to play with us being late."

"It's fine, Charlie, trust me."

"No, I'm riding the bus," Charlie argued, storming off from them.

"Charlie, wait." Jodie said, catching up with her. "What's the real problem?"

Charlie couldn't admit that she was upset that her teacher seemed to favor her. It wasn't fair that everyone seemed to like Jodie. Joey had his science teacher, and they all had Grandma. Why couldn't Charlie have one person to herself?

"He's just becoming a weirdo and I don't like it."

"Yeah, but don't you wanna know about momma?"

"Yeah, but-"

"Come on, Charlie poop, I got this. We'll be home before grandma even knows anything."

Charlie was skeptical as she allowed Jodie to grab her hand as she followed her older sister. There was an eerie feeling running through Charlie's veins that she just couldn't shake. It didn't take being a psychic for Charlie to sense something was about to go wrong.

I'm a Victim of Circumstances (Sample)

"Babies cost money, Terry! If you can't afford to pay a damn water bill, how in the hell are you gonna pay the medical bills, formula, pampers, clothes, and all the baby items that come with having a baby. What are you gonna do, ask mommy and daddy for the money?"

"Okay, so now you want to talk to me like I'm less than a man. I'm out of here," he said, walking off. "You know what though," he added, turning back around, "perhaps you're right. Maybe we shouldn't have kids since my parents can't stand you. They'll probably end up not liking the kids either."

"I don't give a damn, Terry. If your parents choose not to be in our kid's life, then that's on them. I'm not going to beg them to do anything. All I've ever done was been nice to your parents. If they don't like me it's because of something that you're telling them."

"Your actions speak volumes, Lisa."

"Okay, so what have I done to personally fall out of your parents' grace?"

"Look, I'm done with this conversation. I'll pay the damn bill when I get some money," he said, slamming the door on his way out of the house.

Lisa knew that this would be yet another night where Terry would hang out with his friends and get drunk. She was extremely sick of his attitude the past few months and him pressuring her about kids. He had no right to rush her into something that was discussed before they agreed to get married. Lisa called her mom who told Lisa that she shouldn't throw in the towel just yet. Lisa didn't want to throw away three years of marriage, but Terry was seriously pushing her in that direction.

www.ingramcontent.com/pod-product-compliance
Lightning Source LLC
Chambersburg PA
CBHW020153180626
46810CB00004B/1879